From the Ball-Room
to Hell

T. A. Faulkner

Contents

PREFACE. 7

CHAPTER I. FIRST AND LAST STEP. 9

CHAPTER II. FROM THE BALL-ROOM TO THE GRAVE. 18

CHAPTER III. PARLOR DANCING. 26

CHAPTER IV. ABANDONED WOMEN THE BEST DANCERS. 30

CHAPTER V. EQUALLY A SIN FOR BOTH SEXES. 31

CHAPTER VI. THE APPROVAL OF SOCIETY IS NO PROOF AGAINST ....
    THE DEGRADATION. 33

TESTIMONIALS. 38

FROM THE BALL-ROOM
TO HELL

BY

T. A. Faulkner

PREFACE.

You will, my dear reader, find many very plain things between the two covers of this little book; things which will, perhaps, shock your modesty and probably disgust you altogether.

But if you find merely the reading of the facts disgusting, think how much more disgusting is the reality, and how essential that *some* one should portray the evil to the public in a manner impressive and not to be misunderstood.

I have numerous reasons for undertaking this work, chief among them, however, being because I have for many months, felt it to be a duty to my God, and to my fellow-man. Nay, I may put it in a yet more concise form; and simply say, because of a sense of duty to my God, for I believe the two to be inseparable. As the green calyx of the rosebud holds within its embrace everything required to make up the perfect rose in all its beauty of form, texture, tint and perfume, so my duty to my God embraces my whole duty to my fellow-man in all its beauty of kindness, love, and any help or warning I may be able to give, and if that duty shall lead me to speak out boldly and plainly a warning against the evil of a popular amusement, I will boldly and plainly speak, and leave the result with Him whose I am and whom I serve.

Many will, doubtless, object to the book on account of the plainness of the language used; but, my friends, I have endeavored to tell the truth, and to do this on such a subject, does not admit of the use of delicate language. A mild hint at such a fact, clothed in flowery language, would only serve to give a vague impression, and would fall far short of the mission I wish this little book to accomplish, viz.: the opening of the eyes of the people, particularly parents, who are blind to the awful dangers there are for young girls in the dancing academy and ball-room, and of leading some, if possible, to forsake (as I have done) the old unsatisfactory life of selfish pleasure and sinful indulgence and enter upon the purer, nobler and far happier life, which I have found in the service of the Lord.

I do not undertake to write upon a subject of which I am ignorant. There are, perhaps, few people living who have had more practical experience or better opportunities of finding out the evil influences of dancing than myself. I began to dance at the age of twelve and have spent most of my life since that time, until within a few months, in the dancing parlors and academies. For the last six years I have been a teacher of dancing and for several years held the championship of the Pacific Coast in fancy and round dancing. I am also the author of many of the round dances which are the popular fads of the day.

I merely tell you these things to prove to you that I know whereof I speak, and not because I am proud of them. On the contrary, it is the greatest sorrow of my life that I have been so long and in such an influential way connected with an evil which I know to have been the ruin, both of soul and body, to many a bright young life. And if, in the hands of God, I can be the means of leading one-fiftieth as many souls to Christ as I have seen led to a life of vice and crime through the influence of dancing academies with which I have been connected, I shall be more proud than I have ever been of any previous achievements. And if this little book shall, in any degree, help in the accomplishment of this purpose, I shall feel that I am more than repaid for my trouble in its writing, and shall willingly and gladly endure all the harsh criticism and condemnation I know its writing will bring upon me.

T. A. FAULKNER.
FROM THE BALL-ROOM TO HELL.

CHAPTER I.
FIRST AND LAST STEP.

Since my conversion from a dancing master and a servant of the "Evil One" to an earnest Christian and a servant of the Lord Jesus Christ, the question has been repeatedly asked me: "Is there any harm in dancing?"

And letters innumerable have been coming in with questions to the same effect.

The more I mingle with people outside the dancing circle the more forcibly I am made to realize how many there are who are seeking to know the truth concerning the evil of dancing, and how many thousands more who, if they are not seeking that knowledge, certainly ought to have it.

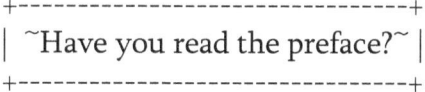

```
+---------------------------------+
| ~Have you read the preface?~ |
+---------------------------------+
```

Let me assure you in the first place that I am well aware that there are many church members and professing Christians who dance; but, if on the strength of this you deem it a safe amusement, come with me for a few evenings, and when you have seen all that I can show you, let your judgment tell you, whether you can, with safety, place your pure, beautiful daughter in the dancing academy or ball-room.

Let us first take an instance from the "select" dancing academy, and thus begin at the root of the matter.

Here is a beautiful young girl. Let me take her for an example.

She is the daughter of wealthy parents; they have been called to mourn the loss of two of their children; and this is their only remaining treasure, their darling, their idol almost, whom they love more than their own lives.

They wish to bestow upon her every accomplishment which modern society demands, so when it is announced that Prof. ---- will open his select dancing academy they hasten to place her under his instruction.

At first she seems shocked at the manner in which he embraces her to teach her the latest waltz.

It is her first experience in the arms of a strange man, with his limbs pressed to hers, and in her natural modesty she shrinks from so familiar a touch. It brings a bright flush of indignation to her cheek as she thinks what an unladylike and indecent position to assume with a man who, but a few hours before, was an utter stranger, but she says to herself: "This is the position every one must take who waltzes in the most approved style--church members and all--so of course it is no harm for me." She thus takes the first step in casting aside that delicate God-given instinct which should be the guide of every pure woman in such matters.

She is very bright and learns rapidly, but a few weeks have passed before she is able to waltz well, and is surrounded by the handsomest and most gallant men in the room, who flatter her until her head is quite turned. She has entirely overcome her delicacy about being embraced in public for half an hour by strange men. In fact she rather likes it now. She wonders all day, before dancing school, if that handsome man who dances so "elegantly" and says such nice things to her, will ask her to dance with him to-night, and finds herself dreaming of how delightful it would be to feel his arm about her.

The evening at last comes; the uninteresting square dances are gone through with, and the music of the waltz begins. Her partner is the Apollo of her day dreams. He presses her close to his breast, and they glide over the floor together as if the two were but one.

When she raises her eyes, timidly at first, to that handsome but deceitful face, now so close to her own, the look that is in his eyes as they meet hers, seems to burn into her very soul. A strange, sweet thrill shakes her very being and leaves her weak and powerless and obliged to depend for support upon the arm which is pressing her to himself in such a suggestive manner, but the sensation is a pleasant one and grows to be the very essence of her life.

If a partner fails, through ignorance or innocence, to arouse in her these feelings, she does not enjoy the dance, mentally styles him a "bore," and wastes no more waltzes on him. She grows more bold, and from being able to return shy glances at first, is soon able to meet more daring ones until, with heart beating against heart, hand clasped in hand, and eyes looking burning words which lips dare not speak, the waltz becomes one long, sweet and purely sensual pleasure.

The more profitable things upon which she has been accustomed to spend her time and thought, lose all attraction for her, and during the time which intervenes between dancing school evenings, she feeds her romantic passion on novels, unfit for any person to read, and which would have been without special interest to her before she entered the dancing school. She spends much thought upon those things which tend to develop her lower nature, for "as a man thinketh, so is he." She has never before had a thought she would not willingly express to her mother. But now she thinks of and discusses with her girl friends of the dancing school, subjects which she would shrink from mentioning to her mother.

O, foolish girl, if she had but remembered that her best friend was her mother, and that thoughts she could not express to her were thoughts in which she should never indulge, what untold sorrow and shame she might have been spared.

She graduates from the academy and is caught into the whirl of society, and her life becomes what is called one round of pleasure--one round certainly of parlor dances, social hops and grand balls with champaign dinners and early goings home (early in the morning, *of course*).

This evening there is to be a ball of unusual grandeur. The last of the season of gaiety, and the closing of the dancing-school term. Our friend will surely be present. Let us attend. What a scene of beauty, gayety and splendor. It must have been of just such scenes the poet wrote:

"There was a sound of revelry by night,
And Belgium's capital had gathered then--
Her beauty and chivalry"--

But see, there is our friend of the dancing academy just entering on the arm of her devoted father. Three months have passed since we first met her. She is much changed, yet one can scarcely see in what the change consists. The face is the same, yet not the same. There is just the shadow of coarseness in it, a little less of frank innocence and true refinement, and a trace, not exactly of ill-health, but a want of freshness. This last is, however, well concealed by the use of cosmetics, and she is still a very beautiful girl, and the fond father's heart swells with pride as he sees the handsomest and most fashionable gentlemen of the ball-room press eagerly forward to ask her hand for the different dances of the evening.

Her father remains for a few of the square dances, but soon retires, knowing that his fair daughter will not want for attention from--gentlemen whose attentions he is sure must be desirable, certainly desirable, why not? Are these admirers not rich and handsome, and do they not move in the highest society. Ah, foolish father, how little he knows of the ways of ball-room society.

But let us turn our attention again to the dancers, at two o'clock next morning. This is the favorite waltz, and the last and most furious of the night, as well as the most disgusting. Let us notice, as an example, our fair friend once more.

She is now in the vile embrace of the Apollo of the evening. Her head rests upon his shoulder, her face is upturned to his, her bare arm is almost around his neck, her partly nude swelling breast heaves tumultuously against his, face to face they whirl on, his limbs interwoven with hers, his strong right arm around her yielding form, he presses her to him until every curve in the contour of her body thrills with the amorous contact. Her eyes look into his, but she sees nothing; the soft music fills the room, but she hears it not; he bends her body to and fro, but she knows it not; his hot breath, tainted with strong drink, is on her hair and cheek, his lips almost touch her forehead, yet she does not shrink; his eyes, gleaming with a fierce, intolerable lust, gloat over her, yet she does not quail. She is filled with the rapture of sin in its intensity; her spirit is inflamed with passion and lust is gratified in thought. With a last low wail the music ceases, and the dance for the night is ended, but not the evil work of the night.

The girl whose blood is hot from the exertion and whose every carnal sense is aroused and aflame by the repetition of such scenes as we have witnessed, is led to the ever-waiting carriage, where she sinks exhausted on the cushioned seat. Oh, if I could picture to you the fiendish look that comes into his eyes as he sees his helpless victim before him. Now is his golden opportunity. He must not miss it, and he does not, and that beautiful girl who entered the dancing school as pure and innocent as an angel three months ago returns to her home that night robbed of that most precious jewel of womanhood--virtue!

When she awakes the next morning to a realizing sense of her position her first impulse is to self-destruction, but she deludes herself with the thought that her "dancing" companion will right the wrong by marriage, but that is the farthest from his thoughts, and he casts her off--"*he* wishes a pure woman for *his* wife."

She has no longer any claim to purity; her self-respect is lost; she sinks lower and lower; society shuns her, and she is to-day a brothel inmate, the toy and plaything of the libertine and drunkard.

How can I picture to you the awful anguish of that mother's heart, the sadness of that father's face, or the dreadful gloom which settles over that once happy home. Neither their love nor their gold can repair the damage done. Their sighs and tears cannot restore that virtue. It is lost, gone forever. Ah, better, yes, infinitely better, would it have been if instead of placing their only darling in the dancing school, they had laid her in the grave by her little sister's side while her soul was pure and spotless.

But how is it with her ball-room Apollo? Does society shun him? Does he pine away and die? Oh, no; he continues in the dancing school, constantly seeking new victims among the pure and innocent.

Like flowers, the choicest ones are plucked first, and most admired, their beauty soon fades and they are cast aside for new ones. Parents, do not discredit my statement. There is no mistake; I know whereof I speak when I say that just such villains as I have described are to be found in, and leaders of, the select dancing school, in the ball room and at the parlor dance, figuring in what is called the best society, as the most refined and highly polished society gentlemen of the day.

Nor is the ball-room scene an imaginary one.

I have seen it, just as described, hundreds, yes, thousands of times, and have known of many and many a case with the same sad ending.

Do not delude yourself, my dear reader, with the thought that such scenes occur only at low public dances. Some of the lowest and most disgusting deeds of which I have had any knowledge, have occurred at and in connection with, the most fashionable parlor dances.

The following infamous deeds were done on one of the principal avenues and at the home of one of the most aristocratic families of this city.

The occasion was a fashionable dance of which I was manager.

There was present the *creme de la creme* of the city's society. Among them two beautiful young women who were actors in the play I am about to put before you. The play is in five acts.

The first scene is of exquisite loveliness. It is a large drawing room, elegant in all its appointments. Its coloring as seen by gas light is soft, rich, and beautifully blended or prettily contrasted. Its pictures are rare bits of art from the brush of the most popular artists of ancient and modern times, and all its ornamentation is forcibly suggestive of culture and refinement. All these things we feel rather than see, for our attention is riveted upon the gay company assembled.

We hear the hum of many voices and see before us scenes of fair women and handsome men, diamonds flash, silks rustle, and no garden of flowers ever displayed a greater variety of rich and dainty color intermingled, or flashed more brightly its gems of morning dew. But hark! From behind that bower of blossoms and evergreens in yonder recess come strains of music which set the little white slipper to tapping out the time as its wearer waits impatiently for the waltz to begin, and now the room presents a scene of whirling, whirling figures.

Notice particularly this couple near us and that one in yonder corner, for I know them well. The ladies are beautiful and respectable.

To be sure, one not accustomed to such scenes would consider them anything but respectably dressed, with their nude arms, neck and partially exposed breast, and tightly clinging skirts which more than suggest the contour of body and limb.

But society and fashion demand such dress; vile men demand it; for them the waltz would be spoiled of half its pleasure if the woman was not as nearly nude as she dare be.

The male companions of the two girls are handsome and fashionable, but of their character not so much can be said, except in condemnation. They are certainly pleasing, and are in every way endeavoring to be so to their young lady companions, and appear to have succeeded very well in their efforts, for, as they whirl over the floor, they gaze into the eyes gloating over them and gleaming with a fury of lust. They allow words to be whispered to them which they would not listen to at any other time; listening now, they come closer still, and in response to a pressure of her hand, his arm tightens its clasp of her waist, and she, losing all restraint, yields herself to the evil passion of the moment. Thus the fury of lustful thought becomes mutual and is mutually enjoyed.

The second scene is in a summer house. Only four characters are required for this act. They are the four we have particularly noticed in the ball-room scene.

This, too, would be a pretty scene, if the pleasure of it were not spoiled for us by the evil we see in it and know may result from it. The summer house, covered with vines and flowers, is in a beautiful garden filled with shrubs and trees. The night is calm and cloudless, and the silvery moon looks sadly down upon the scene through the branches of the trees.

The girls have been invited to retire thither for rest and refreshment. The men have previously arranged with a servant for the refreshments, with plenty of old wine provided for their use, and now they urge the ladies to partake, saying they will feel refreshed and be sustained by it for the remainder of the evening.

After much coaxing and pleading they are induced to take a glass. This accomplished, the men feel that their object is as good as achieved. The wine soon has a visible effect upon the unaccustomed brain, and the girls are easily induced to drink more.

The third and fourth acts are only repetitions of the first and second, and the last and fifth takes place behind the scene. The curtain must fall between us and the going home scene in two hacks to which the half intoxicated girls have been conveyed by brutes in human form.

We only know that these girls are now unable to resist, if they were to try, the deed of shame their male companions are bent upon doing, in that closed carriage, whose driver has been ordered to go slowly, and we know what has taken place, as in after days we see these girls no more in respectable society, although their accomplices still appear as most elegant and highly respectable gentlemen, alias ball-room Apollos.

This tragedy, my friends, was acted out in real life, and is only a sample of hundreds and hundreds of cases of which I have had personal knowledge.

"But," some mothers say, "I know that I can trust my daughter. The waltz may be the means of leading astray some shallow, low-minded girls, and may arouse the lower nature of some of those whose lower nature lies very near the surface, but such girls would go astray anyway. My daughter is a pure, high-minded girl, and I am sure she is trustworthy."

I am glad she is. Keep her so, my friend, ***keep her so***. Do not risk making her otherwise by placing her under the greatest temptation that can possibly come to a girl.

If you place her in the dancing academy or ball-room she cannot and will not remain what you say she now is, and she has but a comparatively small chance of escaping ruin--comparatively only a small chance, I say.

It is a startling fact, but a fact nevertheless, that ***two-thirds of the girls who are ruined fall through the influence of dancing***. Mark my words, I know this to be true. Let me give you two reasons why it is so. In the first place I do not believe that any woman can or does waltz without being improperly aroused, to a greater or less degree. She may not, at first, understand her feelings, or recognize as harmful or sinful those emotions which must come to every woman who has a particle of warmth in her nature, when in such close connection with the opposite sex; but she is, though unconsciously, none the less surely sowing seed which will one day ripen, if not into open sin and shame, into a nature more or less depraved and health more or less impaired. And any woman with a nature so cold as not to be aroused by the perfect execution of the waltz, is entirely unfit to make any man happy as his wife, and if she be willing to indulge in such pleasures with every ball-room libertine, she is not the woman any man wants for a wife. It is a noticeable fact that a man who knows the ways of a ball-room rarely seeks a wife there. When he wishes to marry he chooses for a wife a woman who has not been fondled and embraced by every dancing man in town.

It is also noticeable that after marriage few men care to dance, or to have their wives dance.

The second reason why so many dancing girls are ruined is obvious, when one considers how many fiends there are hanging about the dancing schools and ball-rooms, for this purpose alone, some of them for their own gratification, and others for the living there is to be made from it. I am personally acquainted with men who are professional seducers, and who are to-day making a living in just this way. They are fine looking, good conversationalists and elegant dancers. They buy their admittance to the select (?) dancing school by paying an extra fee, and know just what snares to lay and what arts to practice upon the innocent girls they meet there to induce them to yield to their diabolical solicitations, and after having satisfied their own desires and ruined the girls they entice them to the brothel where they receive a certain sum of money from the landlady, rated according to their beauty and form.

Can you wonder when the degrading, lust-creating influence of the waltz itself is united with the efforts of such vile demons of men as I have, described, that two-thirds of the dancing-school girls are ruined.

It is a greater wonder that any of them escape. The question is often asked: If what you say be true, why do not more of the dancing girls become mothers? I will tell you why. It is because they dance away all fear of maternity. It is the knowledge that the dancing floor *exercise* will relieve if they get into trouble that makes many a woman bold enough to take risks.

Dancing and drinking invariably go together. One rarely finds a dance hall without a bar in it, or a saloon within a few steps of it, and sooner or later those who dance will indulge in drink, which is the devil's best agent in the carrying on of the vile business transacted in, and in connection with, the dance hall.

CHAPTER II.
FROM THE BALL-ROOM TO THE GRAVE.

L et me tell you a true story which will illustrate this point.

It was a Saturday night in the month of December, in the year '91. The girls who toil daily in the stores and shops on Spring street were hastening to their homes after the long week of toil. As they pass along we notice among them the tall, graceful figure of a young woman who seems to be the favorite of the group of girls about her. She is a handsome blonde of nineteen years, with a face as sweet and loving as that of an angel.

She was born in a country town in New England, of respectable parents. Her mother died while she was yet but a little girl, leaving her to the care of a devoted father, who, with loving interest, reared and educated her.

After the completion of her education she entered a printing office, to serve an apprenticeship, but the close confinement, following, as it did, in close proximity to the confinement of the school room, soon undermined her health and a change of climate was prescribed. The father felt he could not part from her even for a few months, but as it seemed for her good, he reluctantly consented to her going to Los Angeles, the "City of the Angels," for a year.

It was a sad day for both when that father and his only daughter parted. Little could he know of the fate that was in store for his pure and loving child in the far West. Little did he think when she kissed him an affectionate farewell, and told him she would return in just one year, that he would never see her smiling face again. Nor did she dream that she was journeying to her doom; that far beyond the mountains she should be laid to rest 'neath the sod of mother earth.

But to return to the scene on Spring street.

As the little group pass up the street her very beautiful face does not escape the notice of the crowd of idlers gathered on the corners gazing impudently at the passers by.

Among these idlers is one of the city's most popular society gentlemen and ball-room devotees, and we hear him mutter to himself as he stares impudently at her pretty face: "Ah, my beauty, I shall locate *your* dwelling place later on. You are too fine a bird to be lost sight of."

He follows her to her lodging, and day by day studies her habits.

He discovers that she goes nowhere except to her daily toil and to church. He visits the church, and finding no opportunity to approach her there, is about to give up the chase when he finds out that the denomination does not condemn dancing.

"Ah, now," he says, "I have you."

He goes to one of the most fashionable dancing schools, where he is well known, and explains his difficulties to the dancing master, who is ever ready to take part in just such dirty work, for it is from the pay for such work that he derives much of the profit of his school.

He sends her a highly colored, gilt-edged card containing a pressing invitation to attend his *select* school.

She does not respond, so he finally sends his wife to press the invitation. The girl, not dreaming of the net that is being woven about her, promises that if her pastor does not disapprove she will attend. Her pastor *does not disapprove*. He tells her that he sees no harm in dancing.

Why does he not see harm in dancing? Has he never been where he *could* see?

She takes it for granted that he *knows*, and acting on his advice attends the school. She is met at the door by the dancing master, who is very polite and so kindly attentive.

The society man who is plotting her ruin is the first person presented to her. He is a graceful dancer and makes the evening pass pleasantly for her, by his kind attentions and praise of her grace in dancing, and when the school is dismissed he escorts her home, which courtesy she accepts, because the dancing master vouches for him, and she thinks that is sufficient. He continues his attentions, and finally invites her to attend, with him, a grand full dress ball to be given at one of the principal hotels. She has never attended a grand ball in her life, and looks forward to this with the greatest pleasure.

The evening at last arrives. Her escort calls for her in an elegant carriage. She looks more beautiful than ever in her pretty, modest evening dress, and he says to himself, "Ah, my Greek Goddess, I shall have the 'belle of the ball' for my victim to-night."

As they enter the ball-room she is quite charmed and dazzled by its splendor and the gaiety of the scene, which is so novel to her.

During the first of the evening her companion finds her more reserved than is to his taste, but he says to himself, only wait, my fair one, until supper time, and the wine will do the work desired.

Twelve o'clock at last comes, and with it the summons to the supper room. Here the well-spread table, the brilliant lights, the flowers, the music and the gay conversation are all sources of the greatest pleasure to the unaccustomed girl, but there is one thing which does not please her. It is the fact that wine is flowing freely and that all are partaking of it. She feels that she can never consent to drink. It is something she has never done in her life. Yet she dares not refuse, for all the others are drinking, and she knows that to refuse would bring upon herself the ridicule of all the party.

She hears her companion order a bottle of wine opened. He pours and offers it, saying, "Just a social glass, it will refresh you." She looks at him as if to protest, but he returns the gaze and hands her the fatal glass, and she has not the moral courage to say no.

As they raise their glasses he murmurs softly, "Here's hoping we may be perfectly happy in each other's love, and that the cup of bliss now raised to our lips may never spill."

One glass and then another and the brain unaccustomed to wine is whirling and giddy. The vile wretch sees that his game is won.

He whispers in her ear many soft and foolish lies, tells her that he loves her, and that if she can return that love, he is hers, and hers alone, so long as life shall last.

She sits tipped back in one chair, with her feet in another, laughs loudly at every poor little joke, and responds, in a silly affectionate manner, to all his words of love, and when he makes proposals to which she would have scorned to listen at any other time, she not only listens but gives consent to all, and does not leave the house that night.

When she awakens next morning, it is in a strange room. Her head whirls, she gazes abstractedly about her and tries to shake off what seems to her to be a horrid dream, but she is brought suddenly to realize that it is no sleeping fancy, but a steam reality, as a low voice by her side says,

"Did you rest easy, my dear?"

"My God!" she fairly shrieks, as the awful truth bursts upon her, "is it possible, or am I dreaming?" and she passes her hand wildly across her face.

"Do not excite yourself, my dear; you are not well. You will feel better presently."

"Better!" she cries, bursting into tears. "Better!! What is life to me now that you have robbed me of my virtue? Oh! that I should have sunken into such depths of sin, and that you, vile man, whom I trusted, should have led me to it."

She tries to rise, but finds herself too weak and dizzy, and falls back heavily upon her pillow.

"Lie still, my love, and when you are able I will let you go. But do not blame me for what has occurred, it was by your own consent. You know I am going to marry you, and all will be well."

"No," she sobs, "all will not be well; nothing will ever be well with me again," and she returns to the room which she has left a few hours before as a bright and happy girl, now broken hearted and on the verge of despair, with a blot upon her young life which nothing on earth can efface. To be sure, he who has brought all this upon her has promised to right the wrong by marriage, but poor consolation it seems to her to have to marry a man whom she feels to be worse than a murderer; even this poor consolation is denied her, however, for the wretch, when he gave the promise, had no thought of fulfilling it. Such trifles as this *he* thinks nothing of. It is the way of most high society men, and when he comes to her again it is not to marry her, but to seek to drag her lower down. She repels him and he is seen by her no more. He has no further use for her.

Days grow to months, and now added sorrow fills her cup of grief to overflowing. She is to become a mother, and the poor girl cries out in bitter anguish: "My God, what shall I do, must I commit murder. Oh, that I had never entered a ball-room."

All her old companions shun her, every one shuns her, even he who led her to her ruin shuns her. She goes to him, hoping he will have compassion upon her, but he meets her with a sneer, calls her a fool, and tells her to commit a yet greater crime than the first, which in her despair she does and "seals the band of death."

She soon became very ill and sank rapidly, and then came a time when she felt that life was short, and that if she wished to leave a message on earth it must be delivered quickly. Having heard of my conversion and that I intended exposing the evils which germinate in the ball-room she sent a messenger requesting me to call immediately.

On entering the house I was led to a couch in a cosy room where lay the beautiful young woman whose pale face showed all to plainly, an amount of sorrow and suffering unwarranted by her years. The countenance of the sufferer brightened as I entered, and she extended her hand saying: "I am so glad you came to see me, so glad to know that you are to expose the evil which buds in the dance hall. Do not delay your work. I have prayed God to spare my life that I might go and warn young girls against that which has made such a sad wreck of my once pure and happy life, for, when I entered dancing school, I was as innocent as a child and free from sin and sorrow, but under its influence and in its association I lost my purity, my innocence, my *all*, but I know that God has forgiven the sin which is sending me to my early grave, where I shall soon be forgotten by all earthly friends.

"Do not grieve for me. I am leaving this dark world for a bright and happy one where sin and sorrow are unknown. Mother is waiting for me there and I am not afraid to go."

We spoke of a hope that she might yet recover, but she only closed her eyes and shook her head slowly.

"No," she said, with considerable effort, "I shall never leave this room alive, never see the green hills of home, never see my father's face, but tell him not to mourn for me, I shall be happy in the arms of Jesus."

"Is there nothing I can do for you?" I asked. "Yes," said she faintly, looking earnestly into my face, "Yes, there is one thing; that which I had hoped I might live to do myself. Promise me that you will do that and I shall die content. Promise me that you will go before the world and speak out a warning against the awful dangers of the dance hall, and try to save young girls from the sin, disgrace and destruction dancing has brought upon me."

I made a solemn promise before God that her request should be complied with.

The dying girl showed unmistakable signs of pleasure at having my faithful promise.

She pressed my hand and said in a voice scarcely audible, "You have seen ball-rooms as they are, my friend, and there is a great and good work before you. May God bless you in it. I seal your promise with death," and before I could speak she was dead and her soul had winged its flight to a heaven of love and peace, where weary hearts shall find perfect love and perfect justice--where not man, but God, judges his children.

I know the man who was the perpetrator of the crime which was the cause of this sad death.

He, to-day, instead of being hung for murder, as he so richly deserved, is a leader in society. His name often appears in the social columns of the daily papers of Los Angeles, as the leader of some fashionable dancing party or Kirmess.

He has been the winner of several prizes in dancing, in fact, is an elegant dancer and is wealthy. These facts gain for him admission to whatsoever society he chooses to enter.

Think, ye parents who have daughters who dance, of their being night after night in the embrace of such men as he, as they most certainly are if they dance much. Such men as he flock to places of dancing for that very purpose.

Some may say that places of dancing are not the only places where such men are to be found. True, but at no other place would they be allowed to take such liberties with your daughters that they may there. This they well know and consequently there are more of them to be found in places of dancing than elsewhere, and it is not the whirling that they go for and enjoy.

How long would dancing be kept up if they were to whirl alone, or if men were to dance with men and women with women? Ah, no; it is not the whirling, but the liberties the waltz affords, which forms its chief attraction.

You, perhaps, think your daughter is in the most select society, and only in such, and will accept only the most respectable gentlemen as partners. But, how are you to know this? How can you be sure that this very man of whom I have been speaking, or another of the same type, is not among those considered the most respectable in the select parlor dances?

You may be perfectly certain that *he* will never publish his own misdeeds, and the girl cannot expose him without making public her own disgrace, so his base deeds go undiscovered and he may still be found at dancing parties or on the street corners engaged in the occupation in which we first met him, viz.: seeking whom he might destroy.

What decent woman, if she knew his real character, would wish to throw herself into the arms of such a man. If she were a true women she would almost rather die than have such a man even touch her, to say nothing of being in his close embrace for the space of a waltz.

Or, what lady would allow any man, in any other public place, except the ballroom, to take the liberties with her that he takes there? Would a lady with a spark of self-respect, at any other place, lay her head upon his shoulder, place her breast against his, and allow him to encircle her waist with his arm, place his foot between hers and clasp her hands in his?

This is the position assumed in waltzing, and I tell you, my friends, that such a position tends, in a greater or less degree, to develop the lower nature of sexes. It cannot be otherwise. It is in perfect accordance with nature. I have heard girls express utter innocence of having any improper emotion aroused by the waltz, but I do not believe this to be strictly true of any girl. If it is, I am sorry for that girl, for she has a sad lack in her nature.

"Male and female, God created them" and placed within them emotions intended to be shared only by man and wife, and if others indulge in those emotions, and continually arouse them by assuming the waltz position, which is only fit for man and wife, they commit a sin against God and nature.

Against God because He has said "Thou shalt not commit adultery," and "I say unto you that whosoever looketh on a woman, to lust after her, hath committed adultery with her already in his heart."

And against nature, because a girl thus constantly aroused, soon breaks her health.

One may work six days in the week and arise fresh every morning, but let him attend a dance for only a few hours each evening and see what will occur. Health and vigor vanish like the dew before the sun.

It is not the exercise which harms the dancer in mind and body, but the coming in such close contact with the opposite sex. Did you ever know a lady who danced to excess to live to be over twenty-five years of age? If she does she is, in most instances, broken in health physically and morally. Doctors claim it to be a most harmful exercise physically for both sexes. The average age of the excessive male dancer is thirty-one.

Beside the harmful exercise there is great danger from the exposure, a girl is so often subjected to in a ball room. She gets in a perspiration during the dance, and as soon as it is over rushes to an open door or window with arms and chest exposed. Is there any wonder that so many women of to-day are unhealthy?

CHAPTER III.
PARLOR DANCING.

Some contend that there is no harm in parlor dancing. How many parents are able to restrict their children to parlor dancing only? Not one in ten thousand.

Dancing is too fascinating, and they who were at first content with parlor dancing soon want something else, and will, for the sake of dancing, go to almost any place.

If private dancing is allowed, and all else strictly forbidden, the child will often deceive his parents and dance at times and in places that they know not of.

I have known young people to be at Sunday night dances, and in low company, when their parents (who only allow parlor dancing) thought they were at church.

They made a practice of going to the church and remaining long enough to get the text of the pastor's discourse, and then going away to spend the time in dancing, and if questioned, they were able to give the text of the evening's sermon, and the trusting parents would not dream of their having been any where but at church.

I only wish that certain parents, who think they are restricting their children to "parlor dancing at home only," could have been with me the night of May 30th, 1892, and seen, as I did, their girls, some of them but twelve or fourteen years of age, dancing in a public saloon, where so much beer had been spilt on the floor that the women had to hold their dresses up to keep them from getting soiled and wet as they danced.

This is usually the result of teaching the child to dance and then restricting them to home dancing. If they once become fascinated with it they must and will, by some means, fair or foul, have more of it than their homes afford.

There are professing Christians who condemn the sale of liquor, advocate the closing of saloons, and frown on Sunday picnics and other amusements, who allow their own children to attend so-called select dancing parties.

In these places are taught the rudiments of an education which may make them graduates of the saloon or the brothel.

I do not say that it **always** does, but I do say that it **often** does.

The safe side is the best side. Keep them from taking the first step to ruin, and they can never take the last.

Where did the majority of the drunkards take their first drink? Where did the gambler play his first card? Where did three-fourths of the women, who are to-day living a life of shame, have a man's arm about them for the first time?

Let me answer.

The first drink of the drunkard was just a social glass.

The first game of the gambler was just a social game.

And three-fourths of the outcasts had a man's arm about them for the first time when they were young girls at a social dance.

There are in San Francisco 2,500 abandoned women. Prof. La Floris says: "I can safely say that three-fourths of these women were led to their downfall through the influence of dancing."

The lot of a Negress in the equatorial forest is not, perhaps, a very happy one, but it is not much worse than that of many a pretty orphan girl in our Christian land.

We talk of the brutalities of the dark, dark ages, and profess to shudder as we read in books of the shameful practices of those times, and yet, here beneath our very eyes, in our ball-rooms and theatres and in many other places, the same hideous abuse, which must be nameless here, flourishes unchecked:

A young penniless girl, if she be pretty, is often haunted from pillar to post by her employer, and if he fails to get her to submit to his diabolical solicitations outside of the ball room, he will manage to get her to attend a dancing school, where he has the **right** to encircle her with his arms and press her to himself until she is inflamed with passion. She hears in the ball room no warning voice, finds no helping hand to guide her in the path of virtue. The only helping hands there are those of which Byron wrote,

"Hands which may freely range in public sight
Were ne'er before--"

and which helps her rapidly down the road to ruin.

When the poor girl is once induced to sacrifice her virtue she is treated as a slave and outcast by the very man who brought her ruin upon her. Her self-respect is gone. Her life becomes valueless to her, and she is swept downward, ever downward, into the bottomless pit of prostitution, and becomes an outcast from her fellow-beings.

But she is far nearer the loving, pitying heart of Christ than all the men who forced her down. And who shall say that Jesus loves her less than He does those who profess to be His followers and the soldiers of His cross, and yet stand silently and idly by while all this fearful wrong goes on.

The matron of a home for fallen women in Los Angeles, says: "Seven-tenths of the girls received here have fallen through dancing and its influence."

Of course, some of these, either from inherited passion or evil education, have deliberately and of free choice entered upon a life of shame; but the great majority do so under the stress of temptation; sometimes because of poverty or chafing against uncongenial employment, with meager wages. They are told that in the profession of prostitution, they can, if they are lucky, make more in a single night than they could by sewing a week.

Can you wonder that many a girl, aroused by the waltz and then lured by such glittering bait, is led to sell herself, soul and body, to those who make use of her and then cast her aside for another?

And yet ball-rooms, where this corruption germinates, flourish and are countenanced by many preachers of the gospel, and attended and encouraged by church members whose pastors have not the moral courage to condemn the evil, for fear of offending some of their members who dance.

The ministers, in a great measure, set the standard of morality in our land, and when they will rise to the occasion and make a long strike, a strong strike, a strike altogether against this ball-room curse, Christian people will strike with them. Then, and not until then, will this evil be wiped out.

It is at the cause and not the effect that the strike must be made.

In some cities the advisability of closing all the houses of prostitution by laws has been discussed.

One might as well try to stop the Mississippi river from flowing by damming it at its mouth, as to try to stop this great stream of vice by closing the doors of the brothel.

To dam the river at its mouth would only cause it to overflow its banks and seek another outlet, and to close the doors of the brothels on one street would only drive them to another.

To stop this great tide of sin we must begin at its source. To close the doors of the brothel, close first the doors of the dancing school.

CHAPTER IV.
ABANDONED WOMEN THE BEST DANCERS.

The most accomplished and most perfect dancers are to be found among the abandoned women. Why? Because they are graduates of dancing schools. If any should wish to ascertain the truth of this let him ask the girls themselves.

I have for several months been working in a Mission of Los Angeles, and where I have before seen causes at work, I have now had ample opportunity of seeing the effect, and I have often heard some of these unfortunate ones cry out in bitter anguish "Would to God that I had never entered a dancing school."

The following 200 were cases of girls who are to-day inmates of the brothel whom I talked with personally. They were frank to answer to my questions in regard to the direct cause of their downfall, and I gathered that these were ruined by:

Dancing school and ball rooms	163
Drink given by parents	20
Willful choice	10
Poverty and abuse	7

	200

I know of a select dancing school where in a course of three months eleven of its victims are brothel inmates to-day.

CHAPTER V.
EQUALLY A SIN FOR BOTH SEXES.

I have, in the preceding pages, spoken chiefly of the harm that comes to women from dancing, and have shown how vile men make use of the privileges the waltz and its surroundings afford to lead once pure girls to impurity and often to crime. But do not think for a moment that because I have here thus spoken, that I hold the women blameless or the dance to the man harmless.

While the woman is more often disgraced in the sight of man, I believe that in the sight of God the sin of dancing is equally a sin for both sexes.

A girl is often ensnared into intoxication and thus into greater sin by vile men, but she is not wholly excusable. If she goes to a ball she must take the consequences. Every woman has a God-given instinct which teaches her right from wrong, and she cannot but know that to indulge in such emotions as the modern waltz fosters is wrong.

It is a horrible fact, but a fact none the less, that it is absolutely necessary that a woman shall be able and willing to reciprocate the feelings of her partner before she can graduate a perfect dancer.

So, even if it be allowed that a woman may waltz virtuously, she cannot, in that case, waltz well.

It matters not how perfectly she knows and takes the steps, she must yield herself entirely to her partner's embrace, and also to his emotions. Until a girl can and will do this she is regarded a scrub by the male experts.

I would that young women who dance could just once be "behind the scenes" when young men meet after an evening's dance to discuss it together, and hear such remarks as "that Miss ---- is a perfect stick. I would not give a fig to dance with her. You can't arouse any more passion in her than you could in a putty man. To waltz with such as she is not what I go for."

Or, another says: "Ah! but that beautiful Miss Smith is a daisy. She is posted. This waltzing is the greatest thing in the world. While you are whirling one of these dear creatures, if you do the thing correctly, you can whisper in her ear things she would shoot you for saying at any other time, but she likes it all the same. They take to it naturally enough if they are properly taught. If you don't know just how it is done go to a dancing master, or any professional dancer. They know, and they will soon let you know. You will soon become a waltzer and thus find out what there is in it."

Such remarks, and worse than these, (remarks unfit to publish even in this plainly written book) are made, my fair young ladies, after the ball, about you by the very young men who, at the dance, you thought so nice and who are so considered. I am ashamed to say in by-gone days, I have been among these young men myself, and I know that to hear them give free expression, loose-tongued, to the lewd emotions and sensual pleasures in which they indulge while in your embrace, is almost as common as the waltz itself.

I repeat what I have said before, that I do not refer to rough, uncultured men, but to those who are looked upon by society as most polished, refined and desirable young men.

If it be true that a woman, however innocent in thought, is the subject of such vile comment, if there is the barest possibility that it may be true, is it not also true that if she is possessed of a remnant of delicacy, she will shrink from exposing herself to such comment, and flee from places of dancing as from a den of vipers?

CHAPTER VI.
THE APPROVAL OF SOCIETY IS NO PROOF AGAINST THE DEGRADATION.

I know that there are many who will contend that I have some selfish or spiteful motive in writing thus strongly in condemnation of the waltz. Many will doubtless claim that the waltz is very moral and healthful, is indulged in by the best people of every land, seemingly tolerated by all, and that he who raises his voice against it does so from other motives than a disinterested desire to warn his fellow-men against it.

I admit that it is indulged in by a great multitude (not of the best) but the most aristocratic society people. But does the fact that society has permitted itself to be carried by storm into a toleration of the modern dance make the dance any less degrading and sinful. No more so, it seems to me, than does the fact of the universal use of alcohol make its effect less harmful or make it any the less a destroyer of homes, happiness and character.

No, its universality does not prove its morality, and it is certain that results prove conclusively its immorality, and all who try to make it out otherwise, are either those who know nothing at all about it and are unwilling to believe that such an evil could be in their midst without their knowledge, or those who know and practice the abominations, but enjoy it far too well to confess what they know. These last will be loudest in their clamor against this book and its author, and in their profession of perfect innocence.

They believe themselves to be the sole possessors of the secret which makes the waltz their pet amusement. They do not mean that their secret shall be divulged, and they seize every opportunity of praising the "beauty and variety" of the waltz.

Its "health giving exercise," "its innocent amusement" and its grace-giving qualities. Grace-giving, forsooth. The grace of the harlot, to my mind, is not the most desirable possession.

I have known many and many a non-dancing mother to encourage her child to learn to dance, because she wanted her to become graceful, and in many a case that daughter has lost grace, health, virtue and all that a woman holds dear. If you have a choice of a saloon for your son, and a so-called select dancing school for your daughter, I beseech you, in the name of God, place your son in the saloon, but keep your daughter out of the dancing school.

If you wish her to become graceful there are schools of physical culture which are much better adapted to the development of health and grace, and much less to the development of vile passions and depraved natures. What I have said before will be no surprise to those who waltz, though, of course, they will feign great surprise, ignorance, and innocence of it all.

But dancing schools are often made use of in a way that is not so well known. Professional thieves often frequent these places. Many of them are perfect dancers and good conversationalists. They appear most respectable and are, of course, so considered, since they are found in the select school, where references are required.

They gain admittance to the school either by practising fraud upon the dancing master, or inducing him to practice fraud upon the public by admitting such a man for a liberal compensation, to what he advertises to be a select school.

When once in a school it is an easy matter to form the acquaintance of the wives and daughters of wealthy men.

To these he makes himself most agreeable, as he well knows how to do, and, if possible, manages by some means or other, to get an invitation to call. If he fails, he makes some excuse to call without an invitation. During his calls he manages, if opportunity presents itself, to seize some valuables; if not he will locate them, to be called for upon some future dark night, and he is quite safe from arrest, for even if suspected he knows that the ladies of the house who have been seen with him in public would only bring disgrace upon themselves by arresting for theft a man upon whose breast they often reclined in public.

This, however, is of small account. If it was the only evil connected with dancing, this book would never have been written. The loss of earthly possessions is of little consequence when compared with the loss of health, happiness, purity and virtue.

I simply tell you this to show you how many evils a dancing master is cognizant of in connection with dancing, that the generality of people know little or nothing about.

Some one has said that few people know better than the dancing master and saloon keeper, how many souls are sent through the port holes of hell between the ages of fourteen and twenty by these two agencies of the devil.

And he is right.

The heart of the dancing master must be even harder than that of the saloon keeper, for while the saloon keeper must witness the harmful and disgraceful indulgence of men, principally, he knows that there is a chance that it may prove only a harmful indulgence.

But the man who can constantly see pure and lovely women being whirled to a disgrace from which she can never recover must have a heart hard indeed. Yet this is what I have witnessed and helped to perpetuate by teaching dancing. Still I heedlessly continued in the business, until something occurred which set me to thinking.

I met on a train, while leaving town, one day a young woman, who, a few months before, had been a member of my select dancing academy. She had been ruined there, and was one of the discarded ones when the school was closed for a few weeks, as all dancing-schools have to be every little while, to get rid of those girls who have met with a fate similar to hers.

I entered into conversation with her and found she could no longer endure being shunned and slighted by all her old companions, and was running away from home. I knew that her parents would be heart broken, and that she, without the protection of a home, would soon sink to utter abandonment, and I tried every persuasion to induce her to return to the home she was leaving. I--who was still teaching the very thing which had been her ruin, now that self-respect and all for which life was worth the living, was lost to her forever--I tried to save her from further degradation.

After I had argued for some time with her she turned fiercely upon me, her once beautiful eyes now filled with a desperation born of despair, and said, with a look and tone of reproach which I shall never forget: "Mr. Faulkner, when you will close your dancing schools and stop this business, which is sending so many girls by swift stages on a straight road to hell, **then, sir**, and not till then, will I think of reform."

I was stirred by her words as I had never been stirred before. But for them I might, perhaps, not have been writing this book to-day. At this I know many may sneer and say that I have myself done more than most men towards the furtherance of the evil I so strongly condemn.

I bow my acknowledgements. I own it all.

"I lived for self, I thought for self,
For self and none beside,
Just as if Christ had never lived.
As though he had never died."

I sinned against heaven and in the sight of God and man, and was in no wise worthy to become a child of him to whom I came ten months ago, and he received me just as I was, all stained with many, many sins, and in his boundless love and mercy he forgave them all.

I feel I cannot close this book without just a word to any of my old companions who may chance to read it, and to others who are leading the life I once led. I want you to forsake that old life I once shared with you and, as I have done, give your-selves into the hands of the Master, Jesus Christ.

You don't know what you are missing of happiness in this world and what you may miss in the world to come. I do not ask you to take my life for an example. That would be a poor example, indeed. We do not have to take any human life for a copy. The life of Christ is the one true example for us all, and I believe that when we stand before, the great Judge of all, the question will not be, **if we have lived as well as this professing Christian or that church member**, but if we have lived our life as nearly like the life of Christ as we could.

And right here let me say a few words to professing Christians and church members who dance. I say "professing" Christians because I believe there is a vast difference between a **Christian** and a "professing" Christian and church member who dances.

To be a **Christian is to be Christlike**, and I believe there is nothing **Christlike** in partaking of such pleasures as have been described in the foregoing pages, even though you indulge no further than the license of the waltz. And even granting (if this were possible) that you only engage in the indecent and suggestive position and motions, without a single sinful thought or feeling, do you believe that your Heavenly Father could say to you, "Well done, thou good and faithful servant. Thou hast spent the evening to my honor and glory. Thou art in the world and not of it. Thou hast done nothing that could cause thy brother to offend, but hast set a good and Godly example. Thou art letting thy light so shine before men that they will see your good works and glorify your Father which is in heaven. Thou art denying thyself and taking thy cross daily and following me. I left my home in glory and lived and suffered and died the death of the crucified that thou mightest take thine ease, dance, drink, and be merry, and then, lay down thy cross and take up thy **crown** in glory to be with thy Savior and be like Him."

"The Son of man cometh at an hour when ye know not."

If he should come and find you at the dance, locked in the embrace of another woman's husband, do you feel that he would consider you ready?

Do you not feel the slightest fear that He would say, "Depart from me, I never knew you?"

Ah, my friends, I should fear it very much. I should fear that to my account would be laid the sin of the harlot.

You say that you dance very properly. What have you to say for those who, looking to you for a Christian example, see that you, a church member, dance, and conclude that there can be no harm in it for them, so they indulge and are ruined by it, and in after days are to be found leading a life of shame in the brothel, all because of your example which led them to take the first step on the downward road?

Do you believe that when you shall both stand before the bar of God for just judgment that none of her sin will be laid to your charge?

Christian friends, a great responsibility rests upon us all, not only to see that we "keep ourselves unspotted from the world," but that we do all in our power to drive from our fair land this awful blot and curse.

TESTIMONIALS.

We have just finished reading Mr. Faulkner's book, called "FROM THE BALL-ROOM TO HELL," and we are profoundly moved by it. We believe every word of it is true, and that his characterization of the demoralization and ruin wrought by the modern dance is none too strongly put.

Surely nothing worse could have been found in Sodom than these Dancing Academies, as a reason why the righteous God sent fire and brimstone and destroyed them all. These exposures are as carefully and delicately written as could be, and yet not fail to be fully understood.

We hope the book will find a wide reading and help to open many eyes that are blind and startle many that are careless, and prove to be a barbed wire fence around many homes of the innocent.

May the Holy Spirit of God bless our Christian brother in his efforts to expose these hot-beds of vice. We advise all pastors and members of our Churches to read this book, and send it to friends.

Signed by the following ministers, of Los Angeles, California.

REV. BRESEE, Pastor Simpson M. E. Church.
REV. D. READ, Pastor First Baptist Church.
REV. H. U. CRABBE, Pastor United Presbyterian.
REV. M. H. STINE, First English Lutheran Church.
REV. A. C. SMITHERS, Temple St. Christian Church.
REV. F. V. FESHER, Vincent M. E. Church.
REV. A. B. PHILLIPS, City and County Missionary.
REV. J. H. COLLINS, Third Congregational Church.

REV. A. ANDERSON, Universalist.
REV. FATHER MORLEY, Catholic Priest.

REV. O. READ writes--"You have photographed the ball-room correctly."

REV. B. FAY MILLS says: May God bless you in your work, and hope that great good will be accomplished by this book. I believe what you say is true. I know of such cases as you have described. It should be read by all Christians.

CAPT. E. R. JENNINGS: "Among those who have spoken in praise of your powerfully written little book, 'From the Ball-Room to Hell,' let my name be enrolled."

REV. E. S. TAYLOR writes: "Last evening I purchased a copy of 'From the Ball-Room to Hell.' I read it through at one sitting, and hasten to thank you for your noble utterance. I know from my own experience that every word is true."

REV. S. E. WILSON, in a long and eulogistic letter, says: "This book fills a vacant niche in the temple of literature, not occupied by sermons or homilies."

PROF. HOMES, ex-dancing master, writes: "This book is founded on facts."

THE REV. FATHER MORLEY, a Catholic Priest of California, writes: "Having carefully read your excellent book, 'From the Ball-Room to Hell,' I cannot forbear expressing my full approval, therefore I cheerfully endorse every line contained therein. You have opened, dear sir, a campaign against public evil. You can send to me one hundred copies, which I shall place in the hands of my followers."

"The author writes evidently under a deep conviction of the truth, and gives a voice of warning in terms that will nigh take away the breath of many parents who read it. We think that every pastor ought to see that one of these books should be placed in the hands of all members of their church."--*California Christian Advocate.*

The lady principal of one of the chief female educational establishments on the Pacific Slope writes: "Myself and lady friends of mine have read the book 'From the Ball-Room to Hell,' and think you have done a noble work, and think it ought to be read by all parents."

PROF. A. T. SULLIVAN, ex-dancing master, says: "Waltzing is the spur of lust."

"We feel pleased that there exists a pen bold enough to denounce the evil complained of in so masterly a manner and in such vigorous English. If we mistake not, it will work great good in the social world."--*Los Angeles Evening Express.*

"This book has created a greater flutter in social circles than anything published within our remembrance. Its pages should receive careful perusal of parents, and the equally careful attention of the young. We believe every word of it is true."--*Los Angeles Times.*

The Codes Of Hammurabi And Moses
W. W. Davies

QTY

The discovery of the Hammurabi Code is one of the greatest achievements of archaeology, and is of paramount interest, not only to the student of the Bible, but also to all those interested in ancient history...

Religion   **ISBN:** *1-59462-338-4*   **Pages:132**
                                             MSRP $12.95

The Theory of Moral Sentiments
Adam Smith

QTY

This work from 1749. contains original theories of conscience amd moral judgment and it is the foundation for systemof morals.

Philosophy **ISBN:** *1-59462-777-0*   **Pages:536**
                                             MSRP $19.95

Jessica's First Prayer
Hesba Stretton

QTY

In a screened and secluded corner of one of the many railway-bridges which span the streets of London there could be seen a few years ago, from five o'clock every morning until half past eight, a tidily set-out coffee-stall, consisting of a trestle and board, upon which stood two large tin cans, with a small fire of charcoal burning under each so as to keep the coffee boiling during the early hours of the morning when the work-people were thronging into the city on their way to their daily toil...

Childrens   **ISBN:** *1-59462-373-2*   **Pages:84**
                                              MSRP $9.95

My Life and Work
Henry Ford

QTY

Henry Ford revolutionized the world with his implementation of mass production for the Model T automobile. Gain valuable business insight into his life and work with his own auto-biography... "We have only started on our development of our country we have not as yet, with all our talk of wonderful progress, done more than scratch the surface. The progress has been wonderful enough but..."

Biographies/ **ISBN:** *1-59462-198-5*   **Pages:300**
                                               MSRP $21.95

The Art of Cross-Examination
Francis Wellman

QTY

I presume it is the experience of every author, after his first book is published upon an important subject, to be almost overwhelmed with a wealth of ideas and illustrations which could readily have been included in his book, and which to his own mind, at least, seem to make a second edition inevitable. Such certainly was the case with me; and when the first edition had reached its sixth impression in five months, I rejoiced to learn that it seemed to my publishers that the book had met with a sufficiently favorable reception to justify a second and considerably enlarged edition. ..

Reference   ISBN: *1-59462-647-2*

Pages:412

MSRP $19.95

On the Duty of Civil Disobedience
Henry David Thoreau

QTY

Thoreau wrote his famous essay, On the Duty of Civil Disobedience, as a protest against an unjust but popular war and the immoral but popular institution of slave-owning. He did more than write—he declined to pay his taxes,   and was hauled off to gaol in consequence. Who can say how much this refusal of his hastened the end of the war and of slavery ?

Law   ISBN: *1-59462-747-9*

Pages:48

MSRP $7.45

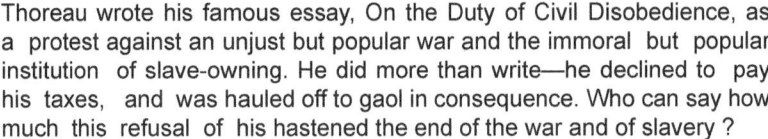

Dream Psychology Psychoanalysis for Beginners
Sigmund Freud

QTY

Sigmund Freud, born Sigismund Schlomo Freud (May 6, 1856 - September 23, 1939), was a Jewish-Austrian neurologist and psychiatrist who co-founded the psychoanalytic school of psychology. Freud is best known for his theories of the unconscious mind, especially involving the mechanism of repression; his redefinition of sexual desire as mobile and directed towards a wide variety of objects; and his therapeutic techniques, especially his understanding of transference in the therapeutic relationship and the presumed value of dreams as sources of insight into unconscious desires.

Psychology   ISBN: *1-59462-905-6*

Pages:196

MSRP $15.45

The Miracle of Right Thought
Orison Swett Marden

QTY

Believe with all of your heart that you will do what you were made to do. When the mind has once formed the habit of holding cheerful, happy, prosperous pictures, it will not be easy to form the opposite habit. It does not matter how improbable or how far away this realization may see, or how dark the prospects may be, if we visualize them as best we can, as vividly as possible, hold tenaciously to them and vigorously struggle to attain them, they will gradually become actualized, realized in the life. But a desire, a longing without endeavor, a yearning abandoned or held indifferently will vanish without realization.

Self Help   ISBN: *1-59462-644-8*

Pages:360

MSRP $25.45

www.**bookjungle**.com *email: sales@bookjungle.com fax: 630-214-0564 mail: Book Jungle PO Box 2226 Champaign, IL 61825*

QTY

The Rosicrucian Cosmo-Conception Mystic Christianity *by Max Heindel* ISBN: *1-59462-188-8* **$38.95**
The Rosicrucian Cosmo-conception is not dogmatic, neither does it appeal to any other authority than the reason of the student. It is: not controversial, but is: sent forth in the, hope that it may help to clear... New Age/Religion Pages 646

Abandonment To Divine Providence *by Jean-Pierre de Caussade* ISBN: *1-59462-228-0* **$25.95**
"The Rev. Jean Pierre de Caussade was one of the most remarkable spiritual writers of the Society of Jesus in France in the 18th Century. His death took place at Toulouse in 1751. His works have gone through many editions and have been republished... Inspirational/Religion Pages 400

Mental Chemistry *by Charles Haanel* ISBN: *1-59462-192-6* **$23.95**
Mental Chemistry allows the change of material conditions by combining and appropriately utilizing the power of the mind. Much like applied chemistry creates something new and unique out of careful combinations of chemicals the mastery of mental chemistry... New Age Pages 354

The Letters of Robert Browning and Elizabeth Barret Barrett 1845-1846 vol II ISBN: *1-59462-193-4* **$35.95**
by Robert Browning and Elizabeth Barrett Biographies Pages 596

Gleanings In Genesis (volume I) *by Arthur W. Pink* ISBN: *1-59462-130-6* **$27.45**
Appropriately has Genesis been termed "the seed plot of the Bible" for in it we have, in germ form, almost all of the great doctrines which are afterwards fully developed in the books of Scripture which follow... Religion/Inspirational Pages 420

The Master Key *by L. W. de Laurence* ISBN: *1-59462-001-6* **$30.95**
In no branch of human knowledge has there been a more lively increase of the spirit of research during the past few years than in the study of Psychology, Concentration and Mental Discipline. The requests for authentic lessons in Thought Control, Mental Discipline and... New Age/Business Pages 422

The Lesser Key Of Solomon Goetia *by L. W. de Laurence* ISBN: *1-59462-092-X* **$9.95**
This translation of the first book of the "Lernegton" which is now for the first time made accessible to students of Talismanic Magic was done, after careful collation and edition, from numerous Ancient Manuscripts in Hebrew, Latin, and French... New Age/Occult Pages 92

Rubaiyat Of Omar Khayyam *by Edward Fitzgerald* ISBN:*1-59462-332-5* **$13.95**
Edward Fitzgerald, whom the world has already learned, in spite of his own efforts to remain within the shadow of anonymity, to look upon as one of the rarest poets of the century, was born at Bredfield, in Suffolk, on the 31st of March, 1809. He was the third son of John Purcell... Music Pages 172

Ancient Law *by Henry Maine* ISBN: *1-59462-128-4* **$29.95**
The chief object of the following pages is to indicate some of the earliest ideas of mankind, as they are reflected in Ancient Law, and to point out the relation of those ideas to modern thought. Religion/History Pages 452

Far-Away Stories *by William J. Locke* ISBN: *1-59462-129-2* **$19.45**
"Good wine needs no bush, but a collection of mixed vintages does. And this book is just such a collection. Some of the stories I do not want to remain buried for ever in the museum files of dead magazine-numbers an author's not unpardonable vanity..." Fiction Pages 272

Life of David Crockett *by David Crockett* ISBN: *1-59462-250-7* **$27.45**
"Colonel David Crockett was one of the most remarkable men of the times in which he lived. Born in humble life, but gifted with a strong will, an indomitable courage, and unremitting perseverance... Biographies/New Age Pages 424

Lip-Reading *by Edward Nitchie* ISBN: *1-59462-206-X* **$25.95**
Edward B. Nitchie, founder of the New York School for the Hard of Hearing, now the Nitchie School of Lip-Reading, Inc, wrote "LIP-READING Principles and Practice". The development and perfecting of this meritorious work on lip-reading was an undertaking... How-to Pages 400

A Handbook of Suggestive Therapeutics, Applied Hypnotism, Psychic Science ISBN: *1-59462-214-0* **$24.95**
by Henry Munro Health/New Age/Health/Self-help Pages 376

A Doll's House: and Two Other Plays *by Henrik Ibsen* ISBN: *1-59462-112-8* **$19.95**
Henrik Ibsen created this classic when in revolutionary 1848 Rome. Introducing some striking concepts in playwriting for the realist genre, this play has been studied the world over. Fiction/Classics/Plays 308

The Light of Asia *by sir Edwin Arnold* ISBN: *1-59462-204-3* **$13.95**
In this poetic masterpiece, Edwin Arnold describes the life and teachings of Buddha. The man who was to become known as Buddha to the world was born as Prince Gautama of India but he rejected the worldly riches and abandoned the reigns of power when... Religion/History/Biographies Pages 170

The Complete Works of Guy de Maupassant *by Guy de Maupassant* ISBN: *1-59462-157-8* **$16.95**
"For days and days, nights and nights, I had dreamed of that first kiss which was to consecrate our engagement, and I knew not on what spot I should put my lips..." Fiction/Classics Pages 240

The Art of Cross-Examination *by Francis L. Wellman* ISBN: *1-59462-309-0* **$26.95**
Written by a renowned trial lawyer, Wellman imparts his experience and uses case studies to explain how to use psychology to extract desired information through questioning. How-to/Science/Reference Pages 408

Answered or Unanswered? *by Louisa Vaughan* ISBN: *1-59462-248-5* **$10.95**
Miracles of Faith in China Religion Pages 112

The Edinburgh Lectures on Mental Science (1909) *by Thomas* ISBN: *1-59462-008-3* **$11.95**
This book contains the substance of a course of lectures recently given by the writer in the Queen Street Hail, Edinburgh. Its purpose is to indicate the Natural Principles governing the relation between Mental Action and Material Conditions... New Age/Psychology Pages 148

Ayesha *by H. Rider Haggard* ISBN: *1-59462-301-5* **$24.95**
Verily and indeed it is the unexpected that happens! Probably if there was one person upon the earth from whom the Editor of this, and of a certain previous history, did not expect to hear again... Classics Pages 380

Ayala's Angel *by Anthony Trollope* ISBN: *1-59462-352-X* **$29.95**
The two girls were both pretty, but Lucy who was twenty-one who supposed to be simple and comparatively unattractive, whereas Ayala was credited, as her Bombwhat romantic name might show, with poetic charm and a taste for romance. Ayala when her father died was nineteen... Fiction Pages 484

The American Commonwealth *by James Bryce* ISBN: *1-59462-286-8* **$34.45**
An interpretation of American democratic political theory. It examines political mechanics and society from the perspective of Scotsman James Bryce Politics Pages 572

Stories of the Pilgrims *by Margaret P. Pumphrey* ISBN: *1-59462-116-0* **$17.95**
This book explores pilgrims religious oppression in England as well as their escape to Holland and eventual crossing to America on the Mayflower, and their early days in New England... History Pages 268

QTY

The Fasting Cure *by Sinclair Upton*   ISBN: *1-59462-222-1*   **$13.95**
*In the Cosmopolitan Magazine for May, 1910, and in the Contemporary Review (London) for April, 1910, I published an article dealing with my experi-
ences in fasting. I have written a great many magazine articles, but never one which attracted so much attention...   New Age/Self Help/Health Pages 164*

Hebrew Astrology *by Sepharial*   ISBN: *1-59462-308-2*   **$13.45**
*In these days of advanced thinking it is a matter of common observation that we have left many of the old landmarks behind and that we are now pressing
forward to greater heights and to a wider horizon than that which represented the mind-content of our progenitors...   Astrology Pages 144*

Thought Vibration or The Law of Attraction in the Thought World   ISBN: *1-59462-127-6*   **$12.95**

by William Walker Atkinson   *Psychology/Religion Pages 144*

Optimism *by Helen Keller*   ISBN: *1-59462-108-X*   **$15.95**
*Helen Keller was blind, deaf, and mute since 19 months old, yet famously learned how to overcome these handicaps, communicate with the world, and
spread her lectures promoting optimism. An inspiring read for everyone...   Biographies/Inspirational Pages 84*

Sara Crewe *by Frances Burnett*   ISBN: *1-59462-360-0*   **$9.45**
*In the first place, Miss Minchin lived in London. Her home was a large, dull, tall one, in a large, dull square, where all the houses were alike, and all the
sparrows were alike, and where all the door-knockers made the same heavy sound...   Childrens/Classic Pages 88*

The Autobiography of Benjamin Franklin *by Benjamin Franklin*   ISBN: *1-59462-135-7*   **$24.95**
*The Autobiography of Benjamin Franklin has probably been more extensively read than any other American historical work, and no other book of its kind
has had such ups and downs of fortune. Franklin lived for many years in England, where he was agent...   Biographies/History Pages 332*

Name	
Email	
Telephone	
Address	
City, State ZIP	

☐ **Credit Card**   ☐ **Check / Money Order**

Credit Card Number	
Expiration Date	
Signature	

Please Mail to: Book Jungle
PO Box 2226
Champaign, IL 61825
or Fax to: 630-214-0564

ORDERING INFORMATION

web*: www.bookjungle.com*
email*: sales@bookjungle.com*
fax*: 630-214-0564*
mail*: Book Jungle PO Box 2226 Champaign, IL 61825*
or PayPal *to sales@bookjungle.com*

Please contact us for bulk discounts

DIRECT-ORDER TERMS

**20% Discount if You Order
Two or More Books**
Free Domestic Shipping!
Accepted: Master Card, Visa,
Discover, American Express

www.ingramcontent.com/pod-product-compliance
Lightning Source LLC
Chambersburg PA
CBHW081203170626
46813CB00009B/3302